Turns Out Teachers Are Humans Too

Turns Out Teachers Are Humans Too

Written by
Kelsey Mills

Illustrated by
Tomasz Pląskowski

NEW YORK

LONDON • NASHVILLE • MELBOURNE • VANCOUVER

Turns Out Teachers Are Humans Too

Published in New York, New York, by Morgan James Publishing. Morgan James is a trademark of Morgan James, LLC. www.MorganJamesPublishing.com

A **FREE** ebook edition is available for you
or a friend with the purchase of this print book.

_____

CLEARLY SIGN YOUR NAME ABOVE

Instructions to claim your free ebook edition:
1. Visit MorganJamesBOGO.com
2. Sign your name CLEARLY in the space above
3. Complete the form and submit a photo
   of this entire page
4. You or your friend can download the ebook
   to your preferred device

ISBN 9781631955662 paperback
ISBN 9781631955679 ebook
Library of Congress Control Number:
2021910409

Cover & Interior Design by:
Christopher Kirk
www.GFSstudio.com

Illustrated by:
Tomasz Pląskowski

with...

Morgan James is a proud partner of Habitat for Humanity Peninsula and Greater Williamsburg. Partners in building since 2006.

Get involved today! Visit
MorganJamesPublishing.com/giving-back

INSPIRED BY KIMBERLY WARD

Have you heard the rumor around the school?
Some kids say teachers have tattoos too!

I think it's silly, a little absurd,
But then I look around, and I see a bird!

I kept my eyes open the rest of the day,
Curiosity filled me, and in me, it stayed.

Hours went by . . . then out in the hall . . .
I saw one! Right there! On Mrs. Mills of all!

I yelled out, "Hey you!" She turned with a start.
I pointed and smiled. What beautiful art!

She turned very red from her toes up to her head.
Putting a finger to her lips, she turned and she fled.

I looked at her very confused—
why was she hiding such good news?

Those bright and joyful roses
might cause some to turn up their noses,

But I think it's wonderful.
They're so bright and colorful!

Mrs. Mills's art tickles my heart.
Turns out . . .

Teachers who are kind, joyous, funny, loving,
and make me feel brand new,

well . . .

not only are they human,
but some have tattoos too!

Kelsey Mills is a former teacher and current writer who resides in Montgomery, Alabama. She is a military spouse and has lived in many states throughout the  country. Kelsey is also a mother and wants to raise her daughter with the understanding that everyone is human and has value in this world.

Tomasz Pląskowski is an illustrator based out of Poland. He has created several pieces for the Museum of the Origins of the Polish State. He has also worked with Polish authors on a variety of children's books. He loves spending summers with his children enjoying holiday.

A free ebook edition is available with the purchase of this book.

To claim your free ebook edition:

1. Visit MorganJamesBOGO.com
2. Sign your name CLEARLY in the space
3. Complete the form and submit a photo of the entire copyright page
4. You or your friend can download the ebook to your preferred device

Morgan James
BOGO™

A **FREE** ebook edition is available for you
or a friend with the purchase of this print book.

CLEARLY SIGN YOUR NAME ABOVE

Instructions to claim your free ebook edition:
1. Visit MorganJamesBOGO.com
2. Sign your name CLEARLY in the space above
3. Complete the form and submit a photo
   of this entire page
4. You or your friend can download the ebook
   to your preferred device

Print & Digital Together Forever.

Snap a photo   Free ebook   Read anywhere

CPSIA information can be obtained
at www.ICGtesting.com
Printed in the USA
BVHW021159300322
632850BV00019B/812